ROBERT
STEVE

THE PAVILION ON
THE LINKS

PENGUIN BOOKS

PENGUIN BOOKS

Published by the Penguin Group. Penguin Books Ltd, 27 Wrights Lane, London
w8 5tz, England. Penguin Books USA Inc., 375 Hudson Street, New York, New
York 10014, USA. Penguin Books Australia Ltd, Ringwood, Victoria, Australia.
Penguin Books Canada Ltd, 10 Alcorn Avenue, Toronto, Ontario, Canada m4v 3b2.
Penguin Books (NZ) Ltd, 182–190 Wairau Road, Auckland 10, New Zealand ·
Penguin Books Ltd, Registered Offices: Harmondsworth, Middlesex, England ·
**This story has been taken from *The Suicide Club and Other Stories* by
Robert Louis Stevenson, published by Penguin Books in 1963.** This edition
published 1995. Printed in England by Clays Ltd, St Ives plc ·

THE PAVILION ON THE LINKS

I

Tells How I Camped in Graden Sea-wood, and Beheld a Light in the Pavilion

I was a great solitary when I was young. I made it my pride to keep aloof and suffice for my own entertainment; and I may say that I had neither friends nor acquaintances until I met that friend who became my wife and the mother of my children. With one man only was I on private terms; this was R. Northmour, Esquire, of Graden Easter, in Scotland. We had met at college; and though there was not much liking between us, not even much intimacy, we were so nearly of a humour that we could associate with ease to both. Misanthropes, we believed ourselves to be; but I have thought since that we were only sulky fellows. It was scarcely a companionship, but a coexistence in unsociability. Northmour's exceptional violence of temper made it no easy affair for him to keep the peace with any one but me; and as he respected my silent ways, and let me come and go as I pleased, I could tolerate his presence without concern. I think we called each other friends.

When Northmour took his degree and I decided to leave the university without one, he invited me on a long visit to Graden Easter; and it was thus that I first became acquainted with the scene of my adventures. The mansion-house of Graden stood in a bleak stretch of country some three miles from the shore of the German Ocean. It was as large as a barrack; and as it had been built of a soft stone, liable to consume in the eager air of the seaside, it was damp and draughty within and half ruinous without. It was impossible for two young men to lodge with comfort in such a dwelling. But there stood in the northern part of the estate, in a wilderness of links and blowing sand-hills, and between a plantation and the sea, a small Pavilion or Belvidere, of modern design, which was exactly suited to our wants; and in this hermitage, speaking little, reading much, and rarely associating except at meals, Northmour and I spent four tempestuous winter months. I might have stayed longer; but one March night there sprang up between us a dispute, which rendered my departure necessary. Northmour spoke hotly, I remember, and I suppose I must have made some tart rejoinder. He leaped from his chair and grappled me; I had to fight, without exaggeration, for my life; and it was only with a great effort that I mastered him, for he was near as strong in body as myself, and seemed filled with the devil. The next morning we met on our usual terms; but I judged it more delicate to withdraw; nor did he attempt to dissuade me.

It was nine years before I revisited the neighbourhood. I travelled at that time with a tilt cart, a tent, and a cooking-stove, tramping all day beside the wagon, and at night, whenever it was possible, gipsying in a cove of the hills, or by the side of a wood. I believe I visited in this manner most of the wild and desolate regions both in England and Scotland; and, as I had neither friends nor relations, I was troubled with no correspondence, and had nothing in the nature of headquarters, unless it was the office of my solicitors, from whom I drew my income twice a year. It was a life in which I delighted; and I fully thought to have grown old upon the march, and at last died in a ditch.

It was my whole business to find desolate corners, where I could camp without the fear of interruption; and hence, being in another part of the same shire, I bethought me suddenly of the Pavilion on the Links. No thoroughfare passed within three miles of it. The nearest town, and that was but a fisher village, was at a distance of six or seven. For ten miles of length, and from a depth varying from three miles to half a mile, this belt of barren country lay along the sea. The beach, which was the natural approach, was full of quicksands. Indeed I may say there is hardly a better place of concealment in the United Kingdom. I determined to pass a week in the Sea-wood of Graden Easter, and, making a long stage, reached it about sundown on a wild September day.

The country, I have said, was mixed sand-hill and links; *links* being a Scottish name for sand which has ceased drifting and become more or less solidly covered with turf. The pavilion stood on an even space; a little behind it, the wood began in a hedge of elders huddled together by the wind; in front, a few tumbled sand-hills stood between it and the sea. An outcropping of rock had formed a bastion for the sand, so that there was here a promontory in the coastline between two shallow bays; and, just beyond the tides, the rock again cropped out and formed an islet of small dimensions but strikingly designed. The quicksands were of great extent at low water, and had an infamous reputation in the country. Close in shore, between the islet and the promontory, it was said they would swallow a man in four minutes and a half; but there may have been little ground for this precision. The district was alive with rabbits, and haunted by gulls which made a continual piping about the pavilion. On summer days the outlook was bright and even gladsome; but at sundown in September, with a high wind, and a heavy surf rolling in close along the links, the place told of nothing but dead mariners and sea disaster. A ship beating to windward on the horizon, and a huge truncheon of wreck half buried in the sands at my feet, completed the innuendo of the scene.

The pavilion – it had been built by the last proprietor, Northmour's uncle, a silly and prodigal virtuoso – presented little signs of age. It was two storeys in height, Italian in design, surrounded by a patch of garden in which nothing had prospered but a few coarse flowers; and looked, with its shuttered windows, not like a house that had been deserted, but like one that had never been tenanted by man. Northmour was plainly from home; whether, as usual, sulking in the cabin of his yacht, or in one of his fitful and extravagant appearances in the world of society, I had, of course, no means of guessing. The place had an air of solitude, that daunted even a solitary like myself; the wind cried in the chimneys with a strange and wailing note; and it was with a sense of escape, as if I were going indoors, that I turned away and, driving my cart before me, entered the skirts of the wood.

The Sea-wood of Graden had been planted to shelter the cultivated fields behind, and check the encroachments of the blowing sand. As you advanced into it from coastward, elders were succeeded by other hardy shrubs; but the timber was all stunted and bushy; it led a life of conflict; the trees were accustomed to swing there all night long in fierce winter tempests; and even in early 5 spring the leaves were already flying, and autumn was beginning in this exposed plantation. Inland the ground rose into a little hill, which, along with the islet, served as a sailing-mark for seamen. When the hill was open of the islet to the north, vessels must bear well to the eastward to clear Graden Ness and the Graden Bullers. In the lower ground, a streamlet ran among the trees, and, being dammed with dead leaves and clay of its own carrying, spread out every here and there, and lay in stagnant pools. One or two ruined cottages were dotted about the wood; and, according to Northmour, these were ecclesiastical foundations, and in their time had sheltered pious hermits.

I found a den, or small hollow, where there was a spring of pure water and there, clearing away the brambles, I pitched the tent, and made a fire to cook my supper. My horse I picketed farther in the wood where there was a patch of sward. The banks of the den not only concealed the light of my fire, but sheltered me from the wind, which was cold as well as high.

The life I was leading made me both hardy and frugal. I never drank but water, and rarely ate anything more costly than oatmeal; and I required so little sleep, that, although I rose with the peep of day, I would often lie long awake in the dark or starry watches of the night. 6 Thus in Graden Sea-wood, although I fell thankfully asleep by eight in the evening I was awake again before eleven with a full possession of my faculties, and no sense of drowsiness or fatigue. I rose and sat by the fire, watching the trees and clouds tumultuously tossing and fleeing overhead, and hearkening to the wind and the rollers along the shore; till at length, growing weary of inaction, I quitted the den, and strolled towards the borders of the wood. A young moon, buried in mist, gave a faint illumination to my steps; and the light grew brighter as I walked forth into the links. At the same moment the wind, smelling salt of the open ocean and carrying particles of sand, struck me with its full force, so that I had to bow my head.

When I raised it again to look about me, I was aware of a light in the pavilion. It was not stationary; but passed from one window to another, as though some one were reviewing the different apartments with a lamp or candle. I watched it for some seconds in great surprise. When I had arrived in the afternoon the house had been plainly deserted; now it was as plainly occupied. It was my first idea that a gang of thieves might have broken in and be now ransacking Northmour's cupboards, which were many and not ill supplied. But what should bring thieves to Graden Easter? And, again, all the shutters had been thrown open, and it would have been more in the character of such gentry to close them. I dismissed the notion, and fell back upon another. Northmour himself must have arrived, and was now airing and inspecting the pavilion.

I have said that there was no real affection between this man and me; but, had I loved him like a brother, I was then so much more in love with solitude that I should none the less have shunned his company. As it was, I turned and ran for it; and it was with genuine satisfaction that I found myself safely back beside the fire. I had escaped an acquaintance; I should have one more night in comfort. In the morning, I might either slip away before Northmour was abroad, or pay him as short a visit as I chose.

But when morning came I thought the situation so diverting that I forgot my shyness. Northmour was at my mercy; I arranged a good practical jest, though I knew well that my neighbour was not the man to jest with in security; and, chuckling beforehand over its success, took my place among the elders at the edge of the wood, whence I could command the door of the pavilion. The shutters were all once more closed, which I remember thinking odd; and the house, with its white walls and green venetians, looked spruce and habitable in the morning light. Hour after hour passed, and still no sign of Northmour. I knew him for a sluggard in the morning; but, as it drew on towards noon, I lost my patience. To say the truth, I had promised myself to break my fast in the pavilion, and hunger began to prick me sharply. It was a pity to let the opportunity go by without some cause for mirth; but the grosser appetite prevailed, and I relinquished my jest with regret, and sallied from the wood.

The appearance of the house affected me, as I drew near, with disquietude. It seemed unchanged since last evening; and I had expected it, I scarce knew why, to wear some external signs of habitation. But no; the windows were all closely shuttered, the chimneys breathed no smoke, and the front door itself was closely padlocked. Northmour, therefore, had entered by the back, this was the natural and, indeed, the necessary conclusion; and you may judge of my surprise, when, on turning the house, I found the back door similarly secured.

My mind at once reverted to the original theory of thieves; and I blamed myself sharply for my last night's inaction. I examined all the windows on the lower storey, but none of them had been tampered with; I tried the padlocks, but they were both secure. It thus became a problem how the thieves, if thieves they were, had managed to enter the house. They must have got, I reasoned, upon the roof of the outhouse where Northmour used to keep his photographic battery; and from thence, either by the windows of the study or that of my old bedroom, completed their burglarious entry.

I followed what I supposed was their example; and, 9

getting on the roof, tried the shutters of each room. Both were secure; but I was not to be beaten; and, with a little force, one of them flew open, grazing, as it did so, the back of my hand. I remember, I put the wound to my mouth, and stood for perhaps half a minute licking it like a dog, and mechanically gazing behind me over the waste links and the sea; and, in that space of time, my eye made note of a large schooner yacht some miles to the north-east. Then I threw up the window and climbed in.

I went over the house, and nothing can express my mystification. There was no sign of disorder, but on the contrary, the rooms were unusually clean and pleasant. I found fires laid, ready for lighting; three bedrooms prepared with a luxury quite foreign to Northmour's habits, and with water in the ewers and the beds turned down; a table set for three in the dining-room; and an ample supply of cold meats, game, and vegetables on the pantry shelves. There were guests expected, that was plain; but why guests, when Northmour hated society? And, above all, why was the house thus stealthily prepared at dead of night? and why were the shutters closed and the doors padlocked?

I effaced all traces of my visit and came forth from the window feeling sobered and concerned.

The schooner yacht was still in the same place; and it flashed for a moment through my mind that this might be the *Red Earl* bringing the owner of the pavilion and his guests. But the vessel's head was set the other way.

2

Tells of the Nocturnal Landing from the Yacht

I returned to the den to cook myself a meal, of which I stood in great need, as well as to care for my horse, whom I had somewhat neglected in the morning. From time to time I went down to the edge of the wood; but there was no change in the pavilion, and not a human creature was seen all day upon the links. The schooner in the offing was the one touch of life within my range of vision. She, apparently with no set object, stood off and on or lay to, hour after hour; but as the evening deepened she drew steadily nearer. I became more convinced that she carried Northmour and his friends, and that they would probably come ashore after dark; not only because that was of a piece with the secrecy of the preparations, but because the tide would not have flowed sufficiently before eleven to cover Graden Floe and the other sea quags that fortified the shore against invaders.

All day the wind had been going down, and the sea long with it; but there was a return towards sunset of the heavy weather of the day before. The night set in pitch dark. The wind came off the sea in squalls, like the firing of a battery of cannon; now and then there was a flaw of rain, and the surf rolled heavier with the rising tide. I was down at my observatory among the elders, when a light was run up to the masthead of the schooner, and showed she was closer in than when I had last seen her by the dying daylight. I concluded that this must be a signal to Northmour's associates on shore; and stepping forth into the links, looked around me for something in response.

A small footpath ran along the margin of the wood, and formed the most direct communication between the pavilion and the mansion-house; and, as I cast my eyes to that side, I saw a spark of light, not a quarter of a mile away, and rapidly approaching. From its uneven course, it appeared to be the light of a lantern carried by a person who followed the windings of the path, and was often staggered and taken aback by the more violent squalls. I concealed myself once more among the elders, and waited eagerly for the new-comer's advance. It proved to be a woman; and as she passed within half a rod of my ambush, I was able to recognize the features. The deaf and silent old dame, who had nursed Northmour in his childhood, was his associate in this underhand affair.

I followed her at a little distance, taking advantage of the innumerable heights and hollows, concealed by the darkness, and favoured not only by the nurse's deafness, but by the uproar of the wind and surf. She entered the pavilion, and, going at once to the upper storey, opened and set a light in one of the windows that looked towards the sea. Immediately afterwards the light at the schooner's masthead was run down and extinguished. Its purpose had been attained, and those on board were sure that they were expected. The old woman resumed her preparations; although the other shutters remained closed, I could see a glimmer going to and fro about the house; and a gush of sparks from one chimney after another soon told me that the fires were being kindled.

Northmour and his guests, I was now persuaded, would come ashore as soon as there was water on the floe. It was a wild night for boat service; and I felt some alarm mingled with my curiosity as I reflected on the danger of the landing. My old acquaintance, it was true, was the most eccentric of men; but the present eccentricity was both disquieting and lugubrious to consider. A variety of feelings thus led me towards the beach, where I lay flat on my face in a hollow within six feet of the track that led to the pavilion. Thence, I should have the satisfaction of recognizing the arrivals, and, if they should prove to be acquaintances, greeting them as soon as they had landed.

Some time before eleven, while the tide was still dangerously low, a boat's lantern appeared close in shore; and my attention being thus awakened, I could perceive another still far to seaward, violently tossed, and sometimes hidden by the billows. The weather, which was getting dirtier as the night went on, and the perilous situation of the yacht upon a lee shore, had probably driven them to attempt a landing at the earliest possible moment.

A little afterwards, four yachtsmen carrying a very heavy chest, and guided by a fifth with a lantern, passed close in front of me as I lay, and were admitted to the pavilion by the nurse. They returned to the beach, and passed me a second time with another chest, larger but apparently not so heavy as the first. A third time they made the transit; and on this occasion one of the yachtsmen carried a leather portmanteau, and the others a lady's trunk and carriage bag. My curiosity was sharply excited. If a woman were among the guests of Northmour, it would show a change in his habits and an apostasy from his pet theories of life, well calculated to fill me with surprise. When he and I dwelt there together, the pavilion had been a temple of misogyny. And now, one of the detested sex was to be installed under its roof. I remembered one or two particulars, a few notes of daintiness and almost of coquetry which had struck me the day before as I surveyed the preparations in the house; their purpose was now clear, and I thought myself dull not to have perceived it from the first.

While I was thus reflecting, a second lantern drew near

me from the beach. It was carried by a yachtsman whom I had not yet seen, and who was conducting two other persons to the pavilion. These two persons were unquestionably the guests for whom the house was made ready; and, straining eye and ear, I set myself to watch them as they passed. One was an unusually tall man, in a travelling hat slouched over his eyes, and a highland cape closely buttoned and turned up so as to conceal his face. You could make out no more of him than that he was, as I have said, unusually tall, and walked feebly with a heavy stoop. By his side, and either clinging to him or giving him support – I could not make out which – was a young, tall, and slender figure of a woman. She was extremely pale; but in the light of a lantern her face was so marred by strong and changing shadows, that she might equally well have been as ugly as sin or as beautiful as I afterwards found her to be.

When they were just abreast of me, the girl made some remark which was drowned by the noise of the wind.

'Hush!' said her companion; and there was something in the tone with which the word was uttered that thrilled and rather shook my spirits. It seemed to breathe from a bosom labouring under the deadliest terror; I have never heard another syllable so expressive; and I still hear it again when I am feverish at night, and my mind runs upon old times. The man turned towards the girl as he spoke; I had a glimpse of much red beard and a nose which seemed to have been broken in youth; and his light eyes seemed shining in his face with some strong and unpleasant emotion.

But these two passed on and were admitted in their turn to the pavilion.

One by one, or in groups, the seamen returned to the beach. The wind brought me the sound of a rough voice crying, 'Shove off!' Then, after a pause, another lantern drew near. It was Northmour alone.

My wife and I, a man and a woman, have often agreed to wonder how a person could be, at the same time, so handsome and so repulsive as Northmour. He had the appearance of a finished gentleman; his face bore every mark of intelligence and courage; but you had only to look at him, even in his most amiable moments, to see that he had the temper of a slaver captain. I never knew a character that was both explosive and revengeful to the same degree; he combined the vivacity of the south with the sustained and deadly hatreds of the north; and both traits were plainly written on his face, which was a sort of danger-signal. In person he was tall, strong, and active; his hair and complexion very dark; his features handsomely designed, but spoiled by a menacing expression.

At that moment he was somewhat paler than by nature; he wore a heavy frown; and his lips worked, and he looked sharply round him as he walked, like a man besieged with apprehensions. And yet I thought he had a look of triumph underlying all, as though he had already done much, and was near the end of an achievement.

Partly from a scruple of delicacy – which I dare say came too late – partly from the pleasure of startling an acquaintance, I desired to make my presence known to him without delay.

I got suddenly to my feet, and stepped forward.

'Northmour!' said I.

I have never had so shocking a surprise in all my days. He leaped on me without a word; something shone in his hand; and he struck for my heart with a dagger. At the same moment I knocked him head over heels. Whether it was my quickness or his uncertainty, I know not; but the blade only grazed my shoulder, while the hilt and his fist struck me violently on the mouth.

I fled, but not far. I had often and often observed the capabilities of the sand-hills for protracted ambush or stealthy advances and retreats; and, not ten yards from the scene of the scuffle, plumped down again upon the grass. The lantern had fallen and gone out. But what was my astonishment to see Northmour slip at a bound into the pavilion, and hear him bar the door behind him with a clang of iron!

He had not pursued me. He had run away. Northmour,

whom I knew for the most implacable and daring of men, had run away! I could scarcely believe my reason; and yet in this strange business, where all was incredible, there was nothing to make a work about in an incredibility more or less. For why was the pavilion secretly prepared? Why had Northmour landed with his guests at dead of night, in half a gale of wind, and the floe scarce covered? Why had he sought to kill me? Had he not recognized my voice? I wondered. And, above all, how had he come to have a ready dagger in his hand? A dagger, or even a sharp knife, seemed out of keeping with the age in which we lived; and a gentleman landing from his yacht on the shore of his own estate, even although it was at night and with some mysterious circumstances, does not usually, as a matter of fact, walk thus prepared for deadly onslaught. The more I reflected, the further I felt at sea. I recapitulated the elements of mystery, counting them on my fingers; the pavilion secretly prepared for guests; the guests landed at the risk of their lives and to the imminent peril of the yacht; the guests, or at least one of them, in undisguised and seemingly causeless terror; Northmour with a naked weapon; Northmour stabbing his most intimate acquaintance at a word; last, and not least strange, Northmour fleeing from the man whom he had sought to murder, and barricading himself, like a hunted creature, behind the door of the pavilion. Here were at least six separate causes for extreme surprise; each part and parcel with the others, and forming all together one consistent story. I felt almost ashamed to believe my own senses.

As I thus stood, transfixed with wonder, I began to grow painfully conscious of the injuries I had received in the scuffle; skulked round among the sand-hills and, by a devious path, regained the shelter of the wood. On the way, the old nurse passed again within several yards of me, still carrying her lantern, on the return journey to the mansion-house of Graden. This made a seventh suspicious feature in the case. Northmour and his guests, it appeared, were to cook and do the cleaning for themselves, while the old woman continued to inhabit the big empty barrack among the policies. There must surely be cause for secrecy, when so many inconveniences were confronted to preserve it.

So thinking, I made my way to the den. For greater security, I trod out the embers of the fire, and lit my lantern to examine the wound upon my shoulder. It was a trifling hurt, although it bled somewhat freely, and I dressed it as well as I could (for its position made it difficult to reach) with some rag and cold water from the spring. While I was thus busied, I mentally declared war against Northmour and his mystery. I am not an angry man by nature, and I believe there was more curiosity than resentment in my heart. But war I certainly declared;

and, by way of preparation, I got out my revolver, and, having drawn the charges, cleaned and reloaded it with scrupulous care. Next I became preoccupied about my horse. It might break loose, or fall to neighing, and so betray my camp in the Sea-wood. I determined to rid myself of its neighbourhood; and long before dawn I was leading it over the links in the direction of the fisher village.

3

Tells How I Became Acquainted with My Wife

For two days I skulked round the pavilion, profiting by the uneven surface of the links. I became an adept in the necessary tactics. These low hillocks and shallow dells, running one into another, became a kind of cloak of darkness for my enthralling, but perhaps dishonourable, pursuit. Yet, in spite of this advantage, I could learn but little of Northmour or his guests.

Fresh provisions were brought under cover of darkness by the old woman from the mansion-house. Northmour, and the young lady, sometimes together, but more often singly, would walk for an hour or two at a time on the beach beside the quicksand. I could not but conclude that this promenade was chosen with an eye to secrecy; for the spot was open only to the seaward. But it suited me not less excellently; the highest and most accidented of the sand-hills immediately adjoined; and from these, lying flat in a hollow, I could overlook Northmour or the young lady as they walked.

The tall man seemed to have disappeared. Not only did he never cross the threshold, but he never so much as showed face at a window, or, at least, not so far as I could see; for I dared not creep forward beyond a certain distance in the day, since the upper floor commanded the bottoms of the links; and at night, when I could venture farther, the lower windows were barricaded as if to stand a siege. Sometimes I thought the tall man must be confined to bed, for I remembered the feebleness of his gait; and sometimes I thought he must have gone clear away, and that Northmour and the young lady remained alone together in the pavilion. The idea, even then, displeased me.

Whether or not this pair were man and wife, I had seen abundant reason to doubt the friendliness of their relation. Although I could hear nothing of what they said, and rarely so much as glean a decided expression on the face of either, there was a distance, almost a stiffness, in their bearing which showed them to be either unfamiliar or at enmity. The girl walked faster when she was with Northmour than when she was alone; and I conceived that any inclination between a man and a woman would rather delay than accelerate the step. Moreover, she kept a good yard free of him, and trailed her umbrella, as if it were a barrier, on the side between them. Northmour kept sidling closer; and, as the girl retired from his advance, their course lay at a sort of diagonal across the beach, and would have landed them in the surf had it been long enough continued. But, when this was imminent, the girl would unostentatiously change side and put Northmour between her and the sea. I watched these manoeuvres, for my part, with high enjoyment and approval, and chuckled to myself at every move.

On the morning of the third day she walked alone for some time, and I perceived, to my great concern, that she was more than once in tears. You will see that my heart was already interested more than I supposed. She had a firm yet airy motion of the body, and carried her head with unimaginable grace; every step was a thing to look at, and she seemed in my eyes to breathe sweetness and distinction.

The day was so agreeable, being calm and sunshiny, with a tranquil sea, and yet with a healthful piquancy and vigour in the air, that, contrary to custom, she was tempted forth a second time to walk. On this occasion she was accompanied by Northmour, and they had been but a short while on the beach, when I saw him take forcible possession of her hand. She struggled, and uttered a cry that was almost a scream. I sprang to my feet, unmindful of my strange position; but, ere I had taken a step, I saw Northmour bareheaded and bowing very low, as if to apologize; and dropped again at once into my ambush. A few words were interchanged; and then, with another bow, he left the beach to return to the pavilion. He passed not far from me, and I could see him, flushed and lowering, and cutting savagely with his cane among the grass. It was not without satisfaction that I recognized my own handiwork in a great cut under his right eye, and a considerable discoloration round the socket.

For some time the girl remained where he had left her, looking out past the islet and over the bright sea. Then with a start, as one who throws off preoccupation and puts energy again upon its mettle, she broke into a rapid and decisive walk. She also was much incensed by what had passed. She had forgotten where she was. And I beheld her walk straight into the borders of the quicksand where it is most abrupt and dangerous. Two or three steps farther and her life would have been in serious jeopardy, when I slid down the face of the sand-hill, which is there precipitous, and, running half-way forward, called her to stop.

She did so, and turned round. There was not a tremor of fear in her behaviour, and she marched directly up to me like a queen. I was barefoot, and clad like a common sailor, save for an Egyptian scarf round my waist; and she probably took me at first for some one from the fisher village, straying after bait. As for her, when I thus saw her face to face, her eyes set steadily and imperiously upon mine, I was filled with admiration and astonishment, and thought her even more beautiful than I had looked to find her. Nor could I think enough of one who, acting with so much boldness, yet preserved a maidenly air that was both quaint and engaging; for my wife kept an old-fashioned precision of manner through all her admirable life – an excellent thing in woman, since it sets another value on her sweet familiarities.

'What does this mean?' she asked.

'You were walking,' I told her, 'directly into Graden Floe.'

'You do not belong to these parts,' she said again. 'You speak like an educated man.'

'I believe I have a right to that name,' said I, 'although in this disguise.'

But her woman's eye had already detected the sash.

'Oh!' she said; 'your sash betrays you.'

'You have said the word *betray*,' I resumed. 'May I ask you not to betray me? I was obliged to disclose myself in your interest; but if Northmour learned my presence it might be worse than disagreeable for me.'

'Do you know,' she asked, 'to whom you are speaking?'

'Not to Mr Northmour's wife?' I asked, by way of answer.

She shook her head. All this while she was studying my face with an embarrassing intentness. Then she broke out:

'You have an honest face. Be honest like your face, sir, and tell me what you want, and what you are afraid of. Do you think I could hurt you? I believe you have far more power to injure me! And yet you do not look unkind. What do you mean – you, a gentleman – by skulking like a spy about this desolate place? Tell me,' she said, 'who is it you hate?'

'I hate no one,' I answered; 'and I fear no one face to face. My name is Cassilis – Frank Cassilis. I lead the life of a vagabond for my own good pleasure. I am one of Northmour's oldest friends; and three nights ago, when I addressed him on these links, he stabbed me in the shoulder with a knife.'

'It was you!' she said.

'Why he did so,' I continued, disregarding the interruption, 'is more than I can guess, and more than I care to know. I have not many friends, nor am I very susceptible to friendship; but no man shall drive me from a place by terror. I had camped in Graden Sea-wood ere he came; I camp in it still. If you think I mean harm to you or yours, madam, the remedy is in your hand. Tell him that my 25 camp is in the Hemlock Den, and tonight he can stab me in safety while I sleep.'

With this I doffed my cap to her, and scrambled up once more among the sand-hills. I do not know why, but I felt a prodigious sense of injustice, and felt like a hero and a martyr; while, as a matter of fact, I had not a word to say in my defence, nor so much as one plausible reason to offer for my conduct. I had stayed at Graden out of a curiosity natural enough, but undignified; and though there was another motive growing in along with the first, it was not one which, at that period, I could have properly explained to the lady of my heart.

Certainly, that night I thought of no one else; and, though her whole conduct and position seemed suspicious, I could not find it in my heart to entertain a doubt of her integrity. I could have staked my life that she was clear of blame, and, though all was dark at present, that the explanation of the mystery would show her part in these events to be both right and needful. It was true, let me cudgel my imagination as I pleased, that I could invent no theory of her relations to Northmour; but I felt none the less sure of my conclusion because it was founded on instinct in place of reason, and as I may say, went to sleep that night with the thought of her under my pillow.

Next day she came out about the same hour alone, and,

as soon as sand-hills concealed her from the pavilion, drew nearer to the edge, and called me by name in guarded tones. I was astonished to observe that she was deadly pale, and seemingly under the influence of strong emotion.

'Mr Cassilis!' she cried; 'Mr Cassilis!'

I appeared at once, and leaped down upon the beach. A remarkable air of relief overspread her countenance as soon as she saw me.

'Oh!' she cried, with a hoarse sound, like one whose bosom has been lightened of a weight. And then, 'Thank God you are still safe!' she added; 'I knew if you were you would be here.' (Was not this strange? So swiftly and wisely does Nature prepare our hearts for these great lifelong intimacies, that both my wife and I had been given a presentiment on this the second day of our acquaintance. I had even then hoped that she would seek me; she had felt sure that she would find me.) 'Do not,' she went on swiftly, 'do not stay in this place. Promise me that you will sleep no longer in that wood. You do not know how I suffer; all last night I could not sleep for thinking of your peril.'

'Peril?' I repeated. 'Peril from whom? From Northmour?'

'Not so,' she said. 'Did you think I would tell him after what you said?'

'Not from Northmour?' I repeated. 'Then how? From whom? I see none to be afraid of.'

'You must not ask me,' was her reply, 'for I am not free to tell you. Only believe me, and go hence – believe me, and go away quickly, quickly, for your life!'

An appeal to his alarm is never a good plan to rid oneself of a spirited young man. My obstinacy was but increased by what she said, and I made it a point of honour to remain. And her solicitude for my safety still more confirmed me in the resolve.

'You must not think me inquisitive, madam,' I replied; 'but if Graden is so dangerous a place, you yourself perhaps remain here at some risk.'

She only looked at me reproachfully.

'You and your father –' I resumed; but she interrupted me almost with a gasp.

'My father! How do you know that?' she cried.

'I saw you together when you landed,' was my answer; and I do not know why, but it seemed satisfactory to both of us, as indeed it was the truth. 'But,' I continued, 'you need have no fear from me. I see you have some reason to be secret, and you may believe me, your secret is as safe with me as if I were in Graden Floe. I have scarce spoken to any one for years; my horse is my only companion, and even he, poor beast, is not beside me. You see, then, you may count on me for silence. So

tell me the truth, my dear young lady, are you not in danger?'

'Mr Northmour says you are an honourable man,' she returned, 'and I believe it when I see you. I will tell you so much; you are right; we are in dreadful, dreadful danger, and you share it by remaining where you are.'

'Ah!' said I; 'you have heard of me from Northmour? And he gives me a good character?'

'I asked him about you last night,' was her reply. 'I pretended,' she hesitated, 'I pretended to have met you long ago, and spoken to you of him. It was not true; but I could not help myself without betraying you, and you had put me in a difficulty. He praised you highly.'

'And – you may permit me one question – does this danger come from Northmour?' I asked.

'From Mr Northmour?' she cried. 'Oh, no; he stays with us to share it.'

'While you propose that I should run away?' I said. 'You do not rate me very high.'

'Why should you stay?' she asked. 'You are no friend of ours.'

I know not what came over me, for I had not been conscious of a similar weakness since I was a child, but I was so mortified by this retort that my eyes pricked and filled with tears, as I continued to gaze upon her face.

'No, no,' she said, in a changed voice; 'I did not mean the words unkindly.'

'It was I who offended,' I said; and I held out my hand

with a look of appeal that somehow touched her, for she gave me hers at once, and even eagerly. I held it for a while in mine and gazed into her eyes. It was she who first tore her hand away, and, forgetting all about her request and the promise she had sought to extort, ran at the top of her speed, and without turning, till she was out of sight. And then I knew that I loved her, and thought in my glad heart that she – she herself – was not indifferent to my suit. Many a time she has denied it in after days, but it was with a smiling and not a serious denial. For my part, I am sure our hands would not have lain so closely in each other if she had not begun to melt to me already. And, when all is said, it is not great contention, since, by her own avowal, she began to love me on the morrow.

And yet on the morrow very little took place. She came and called me down as on the day before, upbraided me for lingering at Graden, and, when she found I was still obdurate, began to ask me more particularly as to my arrival. I told her by what series of accidents I had come to witness their disembarkation, and how I had determined to remain, partly from the interest which had been wakened in me by Northmour's guests, and partly because of his own murderous attack. As to the former, I fear I was disingenuous, and led her to regard herself as having been an attraction to me from the first moment I saw her on the links. It relieves my heart to make this confession even now, when my wife is with God, and already knows all things, and the honesty of my purpose even in this; for while she lived, although it often pricked my conscience, I had never the hardihood to undeceive her. Even a little secret in such a married life as ours, is like the rose-leaf which kept the Princess from her sleep.

From this the talk branched into other subjects, and I told her much about my lonely and wandering existence; she, for her part giving ear, and saying little. Although we spoke very naturally, and latterly on topics that might seem indifferent, we were both sweetly agitated. Too soon it was time for her to go; and we separated, as if by mutual consent, without shaking hands, for both knew that, between us, it was no idle ceremony.

The next, and that was the fourth day of our acquaintance, we met in the same spot, but early in the morning, with much familiarity and yet much timidity on either side. When she had once more spoken about my danger – and that, I understood, was her excuse for coming – I, who had prepared a great deal of talk during the night, began to tell her how highly I valued her kind interest, and how no one had ever cared to hear about my life, nor had I ever cared to relate it, before yesterday. Suddenly she interrupted me, saying with vehemence:

'And yet, if you knew who I was, you would not so much as speak to me!'

I told her such a thought was madness, and, little as we had met, I counted her already a dear friend; but my protestations seemed only to make her more desperate.

'My father is in hiding!' she cried.

'My dear,' I said, forgetting for the first time to add 'young lady', 'what do I care? If he were in hiding twenty times over, would it make one thought of change in you?'

'Ah, but the cause!' she cried, 'the cause! It is' – she faltered for a second – 'it is disgraceful to us!'

4

Tells in What a Startling Manner I Learned that I was not Alone in Graden Sea-wood

This was my wife's story, as I drew it from her among tears and sobs. Her name was Clara Huddlestone: it sounded very beautiful in my ears; but not so beautiful as that other name of Clara Cassilis, which she wore during the longer and, I thank God, the happier portion of her life. Her father, Bernard Huddlestone, had been a private banker in a very large way of business. Many years before, his affairs becoming disordered, he had been led to try dangerous, and at last criminal, expedients to retrieve himself from ruin. All was in vain; he became more and more cruelly involved, and found his honour lost at the same moment with his fortune. About this period North-mour had been courting his daughter with great assiduity, though with small encouragement; and to him, knowing him thus disposed in his favour, Bernard Huddlestone turned for help in his extremity. It was not merely ruin and dishonour, nor merely a legal condemnation, that the unhappy man had brought upon his head. It seems he could have gone to prison with a light heart. What he feared, what kept him awake at night or recalled him from slumber into frenzy, was some secret, sudden, and unlaw-ful attempt upon his life. Hence, he desired to bury his existence and escape to one of the islands in the South Pacific, and it was in Northmour's yacht, the *Red Earl*, that he designed to go. The yacht picked them up clandes-tinely upon the coast of Wales, and had once more deposited them at Graden, till she could be refitted and provisioned for the longer voyage. Nor could Clara doubt that her hand had been stipulated as the price of passage. For, although Northmour was neither unkind nor even discourteous, he had shown himself in several instances somewhat overbold in speech and manner.

I listened, I need not say, with fixed attention, and put many questions as to the more mysterious part. It was in vain. She had no clear idea of what the blow was, nor of how it was expected to fall. Her father's alarm was un-feigned and physically prostrating, and he had thought 33 more than once of making an unconditional surrender to the police. But the scheme was finally abandoned, for he was convinced that not even the strength of our English prisons could shelter him from his pursuers. He had had many affairs with Italy, and with Italians resident in London, in the later years of his business; and these last, as Clara fancied, were somewhat connected with the doom that threatened him. He had shown great terror at the presence of an Italian seaman on board the *Red Earl* and had bitterly and repeatedly accused Northmour in consequence. The latter had protested that Beppo (that was the seaman's name) was a capital fellow, and could be trusted to the death; but Mr Huddlestone had continued ever since to declare that all was lost, that it was only a question of days, and that Beppo would be the ruin of him yet.

I regarded the whole story as the hallucination of a mind shaken by calamity. He had suffered heavy loss by his Italian transactions; and hence the sight of an Italian was hateful to him, and the principal part in his nightmare would naturally enough be played by one of that nation.

'What your father wants,' I said, 'is a good doctor and some calming medicine.'

'But Mr Northmour?' objected Clara. 'He is untroubled by losses, and yet he shares in this terror.'

I could not help laughing at what I considered her simplicity.

'My dear,' said I, 'you have told me yourself what reward he has to look for. All is fair in love, you must remember; and if Northmour foments your father's terrors, it is not at all because he is afraid of any Italian man, but simply because he is infatuated with a charming English woman.'

She reminded me of his attack upon myself on the night of the disembarkation, and this I was unable to explain. In short, and from one thing to another, it was agreed between us, that I should set out at once for the fisher village, Graden Wester, as it was called, look up all the newspapers I could find, and see for myself if there seemed any basis of fact for these continued alarms. The next morning, at the same hour and place, I was to make my report to Clara. She said no more on that occasion about my departure; nor, indeed, did she make it a secret that she clung to the thought of my proximity as something helpful and pleasant; and, for my part, I could not have left her, if she had gone upon her knees to ask it.

I reached Graden Wester before ten in the forenoon; for in those days I was an excellent pedestrian, and the distance, as I think I have said, was little over seven miles; fine walking all the way upon the springy turf. The village is one of the bleakest on that coast, which is saying much:

there is a church in a hollow; a miserable haven in the rocks, where many boats have been lost as they returned from fishing; two or three score of stone houses arranged along the beach and in two streets, one leading from the harbour, and another striking out from it at right angles; and, at the corner of these two, a very dark and cheerless tavern, by way of principal hotel.

I had dressed myself somewhat more suitably to my station in life, and at once called upon the minister in his little manse beside the graveyard. He knew me, although it was more than nine years since we had met; and when I told him that I had been upon a walking tour, and was behind with the news, readily lent me an armful of newspapers, dating from a month back to the day before. With these I sought the tavern, and, ordering some breakfast, sat down to study the 'Huddlestone Failure'.

It had been, it appeared, a very flagrant case. Thousands of persons were reduced to poverty; and one in particular had blown out his brains as soon as payment was suspended. It was strange to myself that, while I read these details, I continued rather to sympathize with Mr Huddlestone than with his victims; so complete already was the empire of my love for my wife. A price was naturally set upon the banker's head; and, as the case was inexcusable and the public indignation thoroughly aroused, the unusual figure of £750 was offered for his capture. He was reported to have large sums of money in his possession. One day, he had been heard of in Spain; the next, there was sure intelligence that he was still lurking between Manchester and Liverpool, or along the border of Wales; and the day after a telegram would announce his arrival in Cuba or Yucatan. But in all this there was no word of an Italian, nor any sign of mystery.

In the very last paper, however, there was one item not so clear. The accountants who were charged to verify the failure had, it seemed, come upon the traces of a very large number of thousands, which figured for some time in the transactions of the house of Huddlestone; but which came from nowhere, and disappeared in the same mysterious fashion. It was only once referred to by name, and then under the initials 'X.X.'; but it had plainly been floated for the first time into the business at a period of great depression some six years ago. The name of a distinguished royal personage had been mentioned by rumour in connexion with this sum. 'The cowardly desperado' – such, I remember, was the editorial expression – was supposed to have escaped with a large part of this mysterious fund still in his possession.

I was still brooding over the fact, and trying to torture it into some connexion with Mr Huddlestone's danger, when a man entered the tavern and asked for some bread and cheese with a decided foreign accent. .

'*Siete Italiano?*' said I.

'*Si, signor,*' was his reply.

I said it was unusually far north to find one of his compatriots; at which he shrugged his shoulders, and replied that a man would go anywhere to find work. What work he could hope to find at Graden Wester I was totally unable to conceive; and the incident struck so unpleasantly upon my mind, that I asked the landlord, while he was counting me some change, whether he had ever before seen an Italian in the village. He said he had once seen some Norwegians, who had been shipwrecked on the other side of Graden Ness and rescued by the lifeboat from Cauldhaven.

'No!' said I; 'but an Italian, like the man who has just had bread and cheese.'

'What?' cried he, 'yon black-avised fellow wi' the teeth? Was he an I-talian? Well, yon's the first that ever I saw, an' I daresay he's like to be the last.'

Even as he was speaking, I raised my eyes, and, casting a glance into the street, beheld three men in earnest conversation together, and not thirty yards away. One of them was my recent companion in the tavern parlour; the other two, by their handsome, sallow features and soft hats, should evidently belong to the same race. A crowd of village children stood around them, gesticulating and talking gibberish in imitation. The trio looked singularly foreign to the bleak dirty street in which they were standing, and the dark grey heaven that overspread them; and I confess my incredulity received at that moment a shock from which it never recovered. I might reason with myself as I pleased, but I could not argue down the effect of what I had seen, and I began to share in the Italian terror.

It was already drawing towards the close of the day before I had returned the newspapers at the manse, and got well forward on to the links on my way home. I shall never forget that walk. It grew very cold and boisterous; the wind sang in the short grass about my feet; thin rain showers came running on the gusts; and an immense mountain range of clouds began to arise out of the bosom of the sea. It would be hard to imagine a more dismal evening; and whether it was from these external influences, or because my nerves were already affected by what I had heard and seen, my thoughts were as gloomy as the weather.

The upper windows of the pavilion commanded a considerable spread of links in the direction of Graden Wester. To avoid observation, it was necessary to hug the beach until I had gained cover from the higher sand-hills on the little headland, when I might strike across, through the hollows, for the margin of the wood. The sun was about setting; the tide was low, and all the quicksands uncovered;

and I was moving along, lost in unpleasant thought, when I was suddenly thunderstruck to perceive the prints of human feet. They ran parallel to my own course, but low down upon the beach instead of along the border of the turf; and when I examined them, I saw at once, by the size and coarseness of the impression, that it was a stranger to me and to those in the pavilion who had recently passed that way. Not only so; but from the recklessness of the course which he had followed, steering near to the most formidable portions of the sand, he was as evidently a stranger to the country and to the ill-repute of Graden beach.

Step by step I followed the prints; until, a quarter of a mile farther, I beheld them die away into the south-eastern boundary of Graden Floe. There, whoever he was, the miserable man had perished. One or two gulls, who had, perhaps, seen him disappear, wheeled over his sepulchre with their usual melancholy piping. The sun had broken through the clouds by a last effort, and coloured the wide level of quicksands with a dusky purple. I stood for some time gazing at the spot, chilled and disheartened by my own reflections, and with a strong and commanding consciousness of death. I remembered wondering how long the tragedy had taken, and whether his screams had been audible at the pavilion. And then, making a strong resolution, I was about to tear myself away, when a gust fiercer than usual fell upon this quarter of the beach, and I saw, now whirling high in the air, now skimming lightly across the surface of the sands, a soft, black, felt hat, somewhat conical in shape, such as I had remarked already on the heads of the Italians.

I believe, but I am not sure, that I uttered a cry. The wind was driving the hat shoreward, and I ran round the border of the floe to be ready against its arrival. The gust fell, dropping the hat for a while upon the quicksand, and then, once more freshening, landed it a few yards from where I stood. I seized it with the interest you may imagine. It had seen some service; indeed, it was rustier than either of those I had seen that day upon the street. The lining was red, stamped with the name of the maker, which I have forgotten, and that of the place of manufacture, *Venedig*. This (it is not yet forgotten) was the name given by the Austrians to the beautiful city of Venice, then, and for long after, a part of their dominions.

The shock was complete. I saw imaginary Italians upon every side; and for the first time, and, I may say, for the last time in my experience, became overpowered by what is called a panic terror. I knew nothing, that is, to be afraid of, and yet I admit that I was heartily afraid; and it was with a sensible reluctance that I returned to my exposed and solitary camp in the Sea-wood.

There I ate some cold porridge which had been left

over from the night before, for I was disinclined to make a fire; and, feeling strengthened and reassured, dismissed all these fanciful terrors from my mind, and lay down to sleep with composure.

How long I may have slept it is impossible for me to guess; but I was awakened at last by a sudden, blinding flash of light into my face. It woke me like a blow. In an instant I was upon my knees. But the light had gone as suddenly as it came. The darkness was intense. And, as it was blowing great gusts from the sea and pouring rain, the noises of the storm effectually concealed all others.

It was, I dare say, half a minute before I regained my self-possession. But for two circumstances, I should have thought I had been awakened by some new and vivid form of nightmare. First, the flap of my tent, which I had shut carefully when I retired, was now unfastened; and, second, I could still perceive, with a sharpness that excluded any theory of hallucination, the smell of hot metal and of burning oil. The conclusion was obvious. I had been awakened by some one flashing a bull's-eye lantern in my face. It had been but a flash, and away. He had seen my face, and then gone. I asked myself the object of so strange a proceeding, and the answer came pat. The man, whoever he was, had thought to recognize me, and he had not. There was yet another question unresolved;

and to this I may say, I feared to give an answer; if he had recognized me, what would he have done?

My fears were immediately diverted from myself, for I saw that I had been visited in a mistake; and I became persuaded that some dreadful danger threatened the pavilion. It required some nerve to issue forth into the black and intricate thicket which surrounded and overhung the den; but I groped my way to the links, drenched with rain, beaten upon and deafened by the gusts, and fearing at every step to lay my hand upon some lurking adversary. The darkness was so complete that I might have been surrounded by an army and yet none the wiser, and the uproar of the gale so loud that my hearing was as useless as my sight.

For the rest of that night, which seemed interminably long, I patrolled the vicinity of the pavilion, without seeing a living creature or hearing any noise but the concert of the wind, the sea, and the rain. A light in the upper storey filtered through a cranny of the shutter, and kept me company till the approach of dawn.

5

Tells of an Interview between Northmour, Clara, and Myself

With the first peep of day, I retired from the open to my old lair among the sand-hills, there to wait the coming of my wife. The morning was grey, wild, and melancholy; the wind moderated before sunrise, and then went about, and blew in puffs from the shore; the sea began to go down, but the rain still fell without mercy. Over all the wilderness of links there was not a creature to be seen. Yet I felt sure the neighbourhood was alive with skulking foes. The light that had been so suddenly and surprisingly flashed upon my face as I lay sleeping, and the hat that had been blown ashore by the wind from over Graden Floe, were two speaking signals of the peril that environed Clara and the party in the pavilion.

It was, perhaps, half past seven, or nearer eight, before I saw the door open, and that dear figure come towards me in the rain. I was waiting for her on the beach before she had crossed the sand-hills.

'I have had such trouble to come!' she cried. 'They did not wish me to go walking in the rain.'

'Clara,' I said, 'you are not frightened!'

'No,' said she, with a simplicity that filled my heart

with confidence. For my wife was the bravest as well as the best of women; in my experience, I have not found the two go always together, but with her they did; and she combined the extreme of fortitude with the most endearing and beautiful virtues.

I told her what had happened; and, though her cheek grew visibly paler, she retained perfect control over her senses.

'You see now that I am safe,' said I, in conclusion. 'They do not mean to harm me; for, had they chosen, I was a dead man last night.'

She laid her hand upon my arm.

'And I had no presentiment!' she cried.

Her accent thrilled me with delight. I put my arm about her, and strained her to my side; and, before either of us was aware, her hands were on my shoulders and my lips upon her mouth. Yet up to that moment no word of love had passed between us. To this day I remember the touch of her cheek, which was wet and cold with the rain; and many a time since, when she has been washing her face, I have kissed it again for the sake of that morning on the beach. Now that she is taken from me, and I finish my pilgrimage alone, I recall our old loving-kindnesses and the deep honesty and affection which united us, and my present loss seems but a trifle in comparison.

We may have thus stood for some seconds – for time passes quickly with lovers – before we were startled by a peal of laughter close at hand. It was not natural mirth, but seemed to be affected in order to conceal an angrier feeling. We both turned, though I still kept my left arm about Clara's waist; nor did she seek to withdraw herself; and there, a few paces off upon the beach, stood Northmour, his head lowered, his hands behind his back, his nostrils white with passion.

'Ah! Cassilis!' he said, as I disclosed my face.

'That same,' said I; for I was not at all put about.

'And so, Miss Huddlestone,' he continued slowly but savagely, 'this is how you keep your faith to your father and to me? This is the value you set upon your father's life? And you are so infatuated with this young gentleman that you must brave ruin, and decency, and common human caution –'

'Miss Huddlestone –' I was beginning to interrupt him, when he, in his turn, cut in brutally:

'You hold your tongue,' said he; 'I am speaking to that girl.'

'That girl, as you call her, is my wife,' said I; and my wife only leaned a little nearer, so that I knew she had affirmed my words.

'Your what?' he cried. 'You lie!'

46   'Northmour,' I said, 'we all know you have a bad

temper, and I am the last man to be irritated by words. For all that, I propose that you speak lower, for I am convinced that we are not alone.'

He looked round him, and it was plain my remark had in some degree sobered his passion. 'What do you mean?' he asked.

I only said one word: 'Italians.'

He swore a round oath, and looked at us, from one to the other.

'Mr Cassilis knows all that I know,' said my wife.

'What I want to know,' he broke out, 'is where the devil Mr Cassilis comes from, and what the devil Mr Cassilis is doing here. You say that you are married; that I do not believe. If you were, Graden Floe would soon divorce you; four minutes and a half, Cassilis. I keep my private cemetery for my friends.'

'It took somewhat longer,' said I, 'for that Italian.'

He looked at me for a moment half daunted, and then, almost civilly, asked me to tell my story. 'You have too much the advantage of me, Cassilis,' he added. I complied of course; and he listened, with several ejaculations, while I told him how I had come to Graden; that it was I whom he had tried to murder on the night of landing; and what I had subsequently seen and heard of the Italians.

'Well,' said he, when I had done, 'it is here at last;   47

there is no mistake about that. And what, may I ask, do you propose to do?'

'I propose to stay with you and lend a hand,' said I.

'You are a brave man,' he returned, with a peculiar intonation.

'I am not afraid,' said I.

'And so,' he continued, 'I am to understand that you two are married? And you stand up to it before my face, Miss Huddlestone?'

'We are not yet married,' said Clara; 'but we shall be as soon as we can.'

'Bravo!' cried Northmour. 'And the bargain? Damn it, you're not a fool, young woman; I may call a spade a spade with you. How about the bargain? You know as well as I do what your father's life depends upon. I have only to put my hands under my coat-tails and walk away, and his throat would be cut before the evening.'

'Yes, Mr Northmour,' returned Clara, with great spirit; 'but that is what you will never do. You made a bargain that was unworthy of a gentleman; but you are a gentleman for all that, and you will never desert a man whom you have begun to help.'

'Aha!' said he. 'You think I will give my yacht for nothing? You think I will risk my life and liberty for love of the old gentleman; and then, I suppose, be best man at the wedding, to wind up? Well,' he added, with an odd smile, 'perhaps you are not altogether wrong. But ask Cassilis here. *He* knows me. Am I a man to trust? Am I safe and scrupulous? Am I kind?'

'I know you talk a great deal, and sometimes, I think, very foolishly,' replied Clara; 'but I know you are a gentleman, and I am not the least afraid.'

He looked at her with a peculiar approval and admiration; then, turning to me, 'Do you think I would give her up without a struggle, Frank?' said he. 'I tell you plainly, you look out. The next time we come to blows –'

'Will make the third,' I interrupted, smiling.

'Ay, true; so it will,' he said. 'I had forgotten. Well, the third time's lucky.'

'The third time, you mean, you will have the crew of the *Red Earl* to help,' I said.

'Do you hear him?' he asked, turning to my wife.

'I hear two men speaking like cowards,' said she. 'I should despise myself either to think or speak like that. And neither of you believe one word that you are saying, which makes it the more wicked and silly.'

'She's a trump!' cried Northmour. 'But she's not yet Mrs Cassilis. I say no more. The present is not for me.'

Then my wife surprised me.

'I leave you here,' she said suddenly. 'My father has been too long alone. But remember this: you are to be friends, for you are both good friends to me.'

She has since told me her reason for this step. As long as she remained, she declares that we two would have continued to quarrel; and I suppose that she was right, for when she was gone we fell at once into a sort of confidentiality.

Northmour stared after her as she went away over the sand-hill.

'She is the only woman in the world!' he exclaimed, with an oath. 'Look at her action.'

I, for my part, leaped at this opportunity for a little further light.

'See here, Northmour,' said I; 'we are all in a tight place, are we not?'

'I believe you, my boy,' he answered, looking me in the eyes, and with great emphasis. 'We have all hell upon us, that's the truth. You may believe me or not, but I'm afraid of my life.'

'Tell me one thing,' said I. 'What are they after, these Italians? What do they want with Mr Huddlestone?'

'Don't you know?' he cried. 'The black old scamp had *Carbonaro* funds on a deposit – two hundred and eighty thousand; and of course he gambled it away on stocks. There was to have been a revolution in the Tridentino, or Parma; but the revolution is off, and the whole wasps' nest is after Huddlestone. We shall all be lucky if we can save our skins.'

'The *Carbonari*!' I exclaimed; 'God help him indeed!'

'Amen!' said Northmour. 'And now, look here: I have said that we are in a fix; and, frankly, I shall be glad of your help. If I can't save Huddlestone, I want at least to save the girl. Come and stay in the pavilion; and, there's my hand on it, I shall act as your friend until the old man is either clear or dead. But,' he added, 'once that is settled, you become my rival once again, and I warn you – mind yourself.'

'Done!' said I; and we shook hands.

'And now let us go directly to the fort,' said Northmour and he began to lead the way through the rain.

6

Tells of My Introduction to the Tall Man

We were admitted to the pavilion by Clara, and I was surprised by the completeness and security of the defences. A barricade of great strength, and yet easy to displace, supported the door against any violence from without and the shutters of the dining-room, into which I was led directly, and which was feebly illuminated by a lamp, were even more elaborately fortified. The panels were strengthened by bars and cross-bars; and these in their turn were kept in position by a system of braces and struts, some abutting on the floor, some on the roof, and others, in fine, against the opposite wall of the apartment. It was at once a solid and well-designed piece of carpentry; and I did not seek to conceal my admiration.

'I am the engineer,' said Northmour. 'You remember the planks in the garden? Behold them!'

'I did not know you had so many talents,' said I.

'Are you armed?' he continued, pointing to an array of guns and pistols, all in admirable order, which stood in line against the wall or were displayed upon the sideboard.

'Thank you,' I returned; 'I have gone armed since our last encounter. But, to tell you the truth, I have had nothing to eat since early yesterday evening.'

Northmour produced some cold meat, to which I eagerly set myself, and a bottle of good Burgundy, by which, wet as I was, I did not scruple to profit. I have always been an extreme temperance man on principle; but it is useless to push principle to excess, and on this occasion I believe that I finished three-quarters of the bottle. As I ate, I still continued to admire the preparations for defence.

'We could stand a siege,' I said at length.

'Ye-es,' drawled Northmour; 'a very little one, per-haps. It is not so much the strength of the pavilion I misdoubt; it is the double danger that kills me. If we get to shooting, wild as the country is some one is sure to hear it, and then

– why then it's the same thing, only different, as they say: caged by law, or killed by *Carbonari*. There's the choice. It is a devilish bad thing to have the law against you in the world, and so I tell the old gentleman upstairs. He is quite of my way of thinking.'

'Speaking of that,' said I, 'what kind of person is he?'

'Oh, he!' cried the other; 'he's a rancid fellow, as far as he goes. I should like to have his neck wrung tomorrow by all the devils in Italy. I am not in this affair for him. You take me? I made a bargain for Missy's hand, and I mean to have it, too.'

'That by the way,' said I. 'I understand. But how will Mr Huddlestone take my intrusion?'

'Leave that to Clara,' returned Northmour.

I could have struck him in the face for this coarse familiarity; but I respected the truce, as, I am bound to say, did Northmour, and so long as the danger continued not a cloud arose in our relation. I bear him this testimony with the most unfeigned satisfaction; nor am I without pride when I look back upon my own behaviour. For surely no two men were ever left in a position so invidious and irritating.

As soon as I had done eating, we proceeded to inspect the lower floor. Window by window we tried the different supports, now and then making an inconsiderable change; and the strokes of the hammer sounded with startling 53 loudness through the house. I proposed, I remember, to make loopholes; but he told me they were already made in the windows of the upper storey. It was an anxious business this inspection, and left me down-hearted. There were two doors and five windows to protect, and, counting Clara, only four of us to defend them against an unknown number of foes. I communicated my doubts to Northmour, who assured me, with unmoved composure, that he entirely shared them.

'Before morning,' said he, 'we shall all be butchered and buried in Graden Floe. For me, that is written.'

I could not help shuddering at the mention of the quicksand, but reminded Northmour that our enemies had spared me in the wood.

'Do not flatter yourself,' said he. 'Then you were not in the same boat with the old gentleman; now you are. It's the floe for all of us, mark my words.'

I trembled for Clara; and just then her dear voice was heard calling us to come upstairs. Northmour showed me the way, and, when he had reached the landing, knocked at the door of what used to be called *My Uncle's Bedroom*, as the founder of the pavilion had designed it especially for himself.

'Come in, Northmour; come in, dear Mr Cassilis,' said a voice from within.

54   Pushing open the door, Northmour admitted me before

him into the apartment. As I came in I could see the daughter slipping out by the side door into the study, which had been prepared as her bedroom. In the bed, which was drawn back against the wall, instead of standing, as I had last seen it, boldly across the window, sat Bernard Huddlestone, the defaulting banker. Little as I had seen of him by the shifting of the lantern on the links, I had no difficulty in recognizing him for the same. He had a long and sallow countenance, surrounded by a long red beard and side whiskers. His broken nose and high cheekbones gave him somewhat the air of a Kalmuck, and his light eyes shone with the excitement of a high fever. He wore a skull-cap of black silk; a huge Bible lay open before him on the bed, with a pair of gold spectacles in the place, and a pile of other books lay on the stand by his side. The green curtains lent a cadaverous shade to his cheek; and, as he sat propped on pillows, his great stature was plainly hunched, and his head protruded till it overhung his knees. I believe if he had not died otherwise, he must have fallen a victim to consumption in the course of but a very few weeks.

He held out to me a hand, long, thin, and disagreeably hairy.

'Come in, come in, Mr Cassilis,' said he. 'Another protector – ahem! – another protector. Always welcome as a friend of my daughter's, Mr Cassilis. How they have rallied about me, my daughter's friends! May God in Heaven bless and reward them for it!'

I gave him my hand, of course, because I could not help it; but the sympathy I had been prepared to feel for Clara's father was immediately soured by his appearance, and the wheedling, unreal tones in which he spoke.

'Cassilis is a good man,' said Northmour; 'worth ten.'

'So I hear,' cried Mr Huddlestone eagerly, 'so my girl tells me. Ah, Mr Cassilis, my sin has found me out, you see! I am very low, very low; but I hope equally penitent. We must all come to the throne of grace at last, Mr Cassilis. For my part, I come late indeed; but with unfeigned humility, I trust.'

'Fiddle-de-dee!' said Northmour roughly.

'No, no, dear Northmour!' cried the banker. 'You must not say that; you must not try to shake me. You forget, my dear, good boy, you forget I may be called this very night before my Maker.'

His excitement was pitiful to behold; and I felt myself grow indignant with Northmour, whose infidel opinions I well knew, and heartily derided, as he continued to taunt the poor sinner out of his humour of repentance.

'Pooh, my dear Huddlestone!' said he. 'You do yourself injustice. You are a man of the world inside and out, and were up to all kinds of mischief before I was born. Your conscience is tanned like South American leather – only you forgot to tan your liver, and that, if you will believe me, is the seat of the annoyance.'

'Rogue, rogue! bad boy!' said Mr Huddlestone, shaking his finger. 'I am no precisian, if you come to that; I always hated a precisian; but I never lost hold of something better through it all. I have been a bad boy, Mr Cassilis; I do not seek to deny that; but it was after my wife's death, and you know, with a widower, it's a different thing: sinful – I won't say no; but there is a gradation, we shall hope. And talking of that – Hark!' he broke out suddenly, his hand raised, his fingers spread, his face racked with interest and terror. 'Only the rain, bless God!' he added, after a pause, and with indescribable relief.

For some seconds he lay back among the pillows like a man near to fainting; then he gathered himself together, and, in somewhat tremulous tones, began once more to thank me for the share I was prepared to take in his defence.

'One question, sir,' said I, when he had paused. 'Is it true that you have money with you?'

He seemed annoyed by the question, but admitted with reluctance that he had a little.

'Well,' I continued, 'it is their money they are after, is it not? Why not give it to them?'

'Ah!' replied he, shaking his head, 'I have tried that already, Mr Cassilis; and alas that it should be so! but it is blood they want.'

'Huddlestone, that's a little less than fair,' said Northmour. 'You should mention that what you offered them was upwards of two hundred thousand short. The deficit is worth a reference; it is for what they call a cool sum, Frank. Then, you see, the fellows reason in their clear Italian way; and it seems to them, as indeed it seems to me, that they may just as well have both while they're about it – money and blood together, by George, and no more trouble for the extra pleasure.'

'Is it in the pavilion?' I asked.

'It is; and I wish it were in the bottom of the sea instead,' said Northmour; and then suddenly: 'What are you making faces at me for?' he cried to Mr Huddlestone, on whom I had unconsciously turned my back. 'Do you think Cassilis would sell you?'

Mr Huddlestone protested that nothing had been further from his mind.

'It is a good thing,' retorted Northmour, in his ugliest manner. 'You might end by wearying us. What were you going to say?' he added, turning to me.

'I was going to propose an occupation for the afternoon,' said I. 'Let us carry that money out, piece by piece, and lay it down before the pavilion door. If the

Carbonari come, why, it's theirs at any rate.'

'No, no,' cried Mr Huddlestone; 'it does not, it cannot belong to them! It should be distributed *pro rata* among all my creditors.'

'Come now, Huddlestone,' said Northmour, 'none of that.'

'Well, but my daughter,' moaned the wretched man.

'Your daughter will do well enough. Here are two suitors, Cassilis and I, neither of us beggars, between whom she has to choose. And as for yourself, to make an end of arguments, you have no right to a farthing, and, unless I'm much mistaken, you are going to die.'

It was certainly very cruelly said; but Mr Huddlestone was a man who attracted little sympathy; and, although I saw him wince and shudder, I mentally endorsed the rebuke; nay, I added a contribution of my own.

'Northmour and I,' I said, 'are willing enough to help you to save your life, but not to escape with stolen property.'

He struggled for a while with himself, as though he were on the point of giving way to anger, but prudence had the best of the controversy.

'My dear boys,' he said, 'do with me or my money what you will. I leave all in your hands. Let me compose myself.'

And so we left him, gladly enough I am sure. The last 59

that I saw, he had once more taken up his great Bible, and with tremulous hands was adjusting his spectacles to read.

7
Tells How a Word was Cried through the Pavilion Window

The recollection of that afternoon will always be graven on my mind. Northmour and I were persuaded that an attack was imminent and if it had been in our power to alter in any way the order of events, that power would have been used to precipitate rather than delay the critical moment. The worst was to be anticipated yet we could conceive no extremity so miserable as the suspense we were now suffering. I have never been an eager, though always a great, reader; but I never knew books so insipid as those which I took up and cast aside that afternoon in the pavilion. Even talk became impossible, as the hours went on. One or other was always listening for some sound, or peering from an upstairs window over the links. And yet not a sign indicated the presence of our foes.

We debated over and again my proposal with regard to the money; and had we been in complete possession of our faculties, I am sure we should have condemned it as unwise; but we were flustered with alarm, grasped at a straw, and determined, although it was as much as advertising Mr Huddlestone's presence in the pavilion, to carry my proposal into effect.

The sum was part in specie, part in bank paper, and part in circular notes payable to the name of James Gregory. We took it out, counted it, enclosed it once more in a dispatch-box belonging to Northmour, and prepared a letter in Italian which he tied to the handle. It was signed by both of us under oath, and declared that this was all the money which had escaped the failure of the house of Huddlestone. This was, perhaps, the maddest action ever perpetrated by two persons professing to be sane. Had the dispatch-box fallen into other hands than those for which it was intended, we stood criminally convicted on our own written testimony; but, as I have said, we were neither of us in a condition to judge soberly, and had a thirst for action that drove us to do something, right or wrong, rather than endure the agony of waiting. Moreover, as we were both convinced that the hollows of the links were alive with hidden spies upon our movements, we hoped that our appearance with the box might lead to a parley, and, perhaps, a compromise.

It was nearly three when we issued from the pavilion. The rain had taken off; the sun shone quite cheerfully. I have never seen the gulls fly so close about the house or approach so fearlessly to human beings. On the very doorstep one flapped heavily past our heads, and uttered its wild cry in my very ear.

'There is an omen for you,' said Northmour, who, like all free-thinkers, was much under the influence of superstition. 'They think we are already dead.'

I made some light rejoinder, but it was with half my heart; for the circumstance had impressed me.

A yard or two before the gate, on a patch of smooth turf, we set down the dispatch-box; and Northmour waved a white handkerchief over his head. Nothing replied. We raised our voices, and cried aloud in Italian that we were there as ambassadors to arrange the quarrel; but the stillness remained unbroken save by the seagulls and the surf. I had a weight at my heart when we desisted; and I saw that even Northmour was unusually pale. He looked over his shoulder nervously, as though he feared that some one had crept between him and the pavilion door.

'By God,' he said in a whisper, 'this is too much for me!'

I replied in the same key: 'Suppose there should be none, after all?'

'Look there,' he returned, nodding with his head, as though he had been afraid to point.

I glanced in the direction indicated; and there, from the

northern quarter of the Sea-wood, beheld a thin column of smoke rising steadily against the now cloudless sky.

'Northmour,' I said (we still continued to talk in whispers), 'it is not possible to endure this suspense. I prefer death fifty times over. Stay you here to watch the pavilion; I will go forward and make sure, if I have to walk right into their camp.'

He looked once again all round him with puckered eyes, and then nodded assentingly to my proposal.

My heart beat like a sledge-hammer as I set out walking rapidly in the direction of the smoke; and, though up to that moment I had felt chill and shivering, I was suddenly conscious of a glow of heat over all my body. The ground in this direction was very uneven; a hundred men might have lain hidden in as many square yards about my path. But I had not practised the business in vain, chose such routes as cut at the very root of concealment, and, by keeping along the most convenient ridges, commanded several hollows at a time. It was not long before I was rewarded for my caution. Coming suddenly on to a mound somewhat more elevated than the surrounding hummocks, I saw, not thirty yards away, a man bent almost double, and running as fast as his attitude permitted, along the bottom of a gully. I had dislodged one of the spies from his ambush. As soon as I sighted him, I called loudly both in English and Italian and he, seeing concealment was no longer possible, straightened himself out, leaped from the gully, and made off as straight as an arrow for the borders of the wood.

It was none of my business to pursue; I had learned what I wanted – that we were beleaguered and watched in the pavilion; and I returned at once, and walking as nearly as possible in my old footsteps, to where Northmour awaited me beside the dispatch-box. He was even paler than when I had left him, and his voice shook a little.

'Could you see what he was like?' he asked.

'He kept his back turned,' I replied.

'Let us get into the house, Frank. I don't think I'm a coward, but I can stand no more of this,' he whispered.

All was still and sunshiny about the pavilion as we turned to re-enter it; even the gulls had flown in a wider circuit, and were seen flickering along the beach and sand-hills; and this loneliness terrified me more than a regiment under arms. It was not until the door was barricaded that I could draw a full inspiration and relieve the weight that lay upon my bosom. Northmour and I exchanged a steady glance; and I suppose each made his own reflections on the white and startled aspect of the other.

'You were right,' I said. 'All is over. Shake hands, old man, for the last time.'

'Yes,' replied he, 'I will shake hands for, as sure as I am

here, I bear no malice. But remember, if, by some impossible accident we should give the slip to these blackguards, I'll take the upper hand of you by fair or foul.'

'Oh,' said I, 'you weary me!'

He seemed hurt, and walked away in silence to the foot of the stairs, where he paused.

'You do not understand,' said he. 'I am not a swindler, and I guard myself; that is all. It may weary you or not, Mr Cassilis, I do not care a rush; I speak for my own satisfaction, and not for your amusement. You had better go upstairs and court the girl; for my part, I stay here.'

'And I stay with you,' I returned. 'Do you think I would steal a march, even with your permission?'

'Frank,' he said, smiling, 'it's a pity you are an ass, for you have the makings of a man. I think I must be *fey* today; you cannot irritate me even when you try. Do you know,' he continued softly, 'I think we are the two most miserable men in England, you and I! we have got on to thirty without wife or child, or so much as a shop to look after – poor, pitiful, lost devils, both! And now we clash about a girl! As if there were not several millions in the United Kingdom! Ah, Frank, Frank, the one who loses this throw, be it you or me, he has my pity! It were better for him – how does the Bible say? – that a millstone were hanged about his neck and he were cast into the depth of the sea. Let us take a drink,' he concluded suddenly, but without any levity of tone.

I was touched by his words, and consented. He sat down on the table in the dining-room, and held up the glass of sherry to his eye.

'If you beat me, Frank,' he said, 'I shall take to drink. What will you do, if it goes the other way?'

'God knows,' I returned.

'Well,' said he, 'here is a toast in the meantime: "*Italia irredenta!*"'

The remainder of the day was passed in the same dreadful tedium and suspense. I laid the table for dinner, while Northmour and Clara prepared the meal together in the kitchen. I could hear their talk as I went to and fro, and was surprised to find it ran all the time upon myself. Northmour again bracketed us together, and rallied Clara on a choice of husbands; but he continued to speak of me with some feeling, and uttered nothing to my prejudice unless he included himself in the condemnation. This awakened a sense of gratitude in my heart which combined, with the immediateness of our peril, to fill my eyes with tears. After all, I thought – and perhaps the thought was laughably vain – we were here three very noble human beings to perish in defence of a thieving banker.

Before we sat down to table, I looked forth from an upstairs window. The day was beginning to decline; the links were utterly deserted; the dispatch-box still lay untouched where we had left it hours before.

Mr Huddlestone, in a long yellow dressing-gown, took one end of the table, Clara the other; while Northmour and I faced each other from the sides. The lamp was brightly trimmed; the wine was good; the viands, although mostly cold, excellent of their sort. We seemed to have agreed tacitly; all reference to the impending catastrophe was carefully avoided; and, considering our tragic circumstances, we made a merrier party than could have been expected. From time to time, it is true, Northmour or I would rise from the table and make a round of the defences; and, on each of these occasions, Mr Huddlestone was recalled to a sense of his tragic predicament, glanced up with ghastly eyes, and bore for an instant on his countenance the stamp of terror. But he hastened to empty his glass, wiped his forehead with his handkerchief, and joined again in the conversation.

I was astonished at the wit and information he displayed. Mr Huddlestone's was certainly no ordinary character; he had read and observed for himself; his gifts were sound; and, though I could never have learned to love the man, I began to understand his success in business, and the great respect in which he had been held before his failure. He had, above all, the talent of society; and though I never heard him speak but on this one and most unfavourable occasion, I set him down among the most brilliant conversationalists I ever met.

He was relating with great gusto, and seemingly no feeling of shame, the manoeuvres of a scoundrelly commission merchant whom he had known and studied in his youth, and we were all listening with an odd mixture of mirth and embarrassment, when our little party was brought abruptly to an end in the most startling manner.

A noise like that of a wet finger on the window-pane interrupted Huddlestone's tale; and in an instant we were all four as white as paper, and sat tongue-tied and motionless round the table.

'A snail,' I said at last; for I had heard that these animals make a noise somewhat similar in character.

'Snail be damned!' said Northmour. 'Hush!'

The same sound was repeated twice at regular intervals; and then a formidable voice shouted through the shutters the Italian word '*Traditore!*'

Mr Huddlestone threw his head in the air; his eyelids quivered; next moment he fell insensible below the table. Northmour and I had each run to the armoury and seized a gun. Clara was on her feet with her hand at her throat.

So we stood waiting, for we thought the hour of attack was certainly come; but second passed after second, and all but the surf remained silent in the neighbourhood of the pavilion.

'Quick,' said Northmour; 'upstairs with him before they come.'

8

Tells of the Last of the Tall Man

Somehow or other, by hook and crook, and between the three of us, we got Bernard Huddlestone bundled upstairs and laid upon the bed in *My Uncle's Room*. During the whole process, which was rough enough, he gave no sign of consciousness, and he remained, as we had thrown him, without changing the position of a finger. His daughter opened his shirt and began to wet his head and bosom; while Northmour and I ran to the window. The weather continued clear; the moon, which was now about full, had risen and shed a very clear light upon the links; yet, strain our eyes as we might, we could distinguish nothing moving. A few dark spots, more or less, on the uneven expanse were not to be identified; they might be crouching men, they might be shadows; it was impossible to be sure.

'Thank God,' said Northmour, 'Aggie is not coming tonight.'

Aggie was the name of the old nurse; he had not thought of her till now; but that he should think of her at all, was a trait that surprised me in the man.

We were again reduced to waiting. Northmour went to the fireplace and spread his hands before the red embers, as if he were cold. I followed him mechanically with my eyes, and in so doing turned my back upon the window. At that moment a very faint report was audible from without, and a ball shivered a pane of glass, and buried itself in the shutter two inches from my head. I heard Clara scream; and though I whipped instantly out of range and into a corner, she was there, so to speak, before me, beseeching to know if I were hurt. I felt that I could stand to be shot at every day and all day long, with such marks of solicitude for a reward; and I continued to reassure her, with the tenderest caresses and in complete forgetfulness of our situation, till the voice of Northmour recalled me to myself.

'An air-gun,' he said. 'They wish to make no noise.'

I put Clara aside, and looked at him. He was standing with his back to the fire and his hands clasped behind him; and I knew, by the black look on his face, that passion was boiling within. I had seen just such a look before he attacked me, that March night, in the adjoining chamber; and, though I could make every allowance for his anger, I confess I trembled for the consequences. He gazed straight before him; but he could see us with the tail of his eye, and his temper kept rising like a gale of wind. With regular battle awaiting us outside, this prospect of an internecine strife within the walls began to daunt me.

Suddenly, as I was thus closely watching his expression and prepared against the worst, I saw a change, a flash, a look of relief upon his face. He took up the lamp which stood beside him on the table, and turned to us with an air of some excitement.

'There is one point that we must know,' said he. 'Are they going to butcher the lot of us, or only Huddlestone? Did they take you for him, or fire at you for your own *beaux yeux*?'

'They took me for him, for certain,' I replied. 'I am near as tall and my head is fair.'

'I am going to make sure,' returned Northmour; and he stepped up to the window, holding the lamp above his head, and stood there, quietly affronting death, for half a minute.

Clara sought to rush forward and pull him from the place of danger; but I had the pardonable selfishness to hold her back by force.

'Yes,' said Northmour, turning coolly from the window; 'it's only Huddlestone they want.'

'Oh, Mr Northmour!' cried Clara; but found no more to add; the temerity she had just witnessed seeming beyond the reach of words.

He, on his part, looked at me, cocking his head, with a fire of triumph in his eyes; and I understood at once that he had thus hazarded his life, merely to attract Clara's notice, and depose me from my position as the hero of the hour. He snapped his fingers.

'The fire is only beginning,' said he. 'When they warm up to their work, they won't be so particular.'

A voice was now heard hailing us from the entrance. From the window we could see the figure of a man in the moonlight; he stood motionless, his face uplifted to ours, and a rag of something white on his extended arm; and as we looked right down upon him, though he was a good many yards distant on the links, we could see the moonlight glitter on his eyes.

He opened his lips again, and spoke for some minutes on end, in a key so loud that he might have been heard in every corner of the pavilion, and as far away as the borders of the wood. It was the same voice that had already shouted '*Traditore!*' through the shutters of the dining-room; this time it made a complete and clear statement. If the traitor 'Huddlestone' were given up, all others should be spared; if not, no one should escape to tell the tale.

'Well, Huddlestone, what do you say to that?' asked Northmour, turning to the bed.

Up to that moment the banker had given no sign of life and I, at least, had supposed him to be still lying in a faint; but he replied at once, and in such tones as I have never heard elsewhere, save from a delirious patient, adjured and besought us not to desert him. It was the most hideous and abject performance that my imagination can conceive.

'Enough,' cried Northmour; and then he threw open the window, leaned out into the night, and in a tone of exultation, and with a total forgetfulness of what was due to the presence of a lady, poured out upon the ambassador a string of the most abominable raillery both in English and Italian, and bade him be gone where he had come from. I believe that nothing so delighted Northmour at that moment as the thought that we must all infallibly perish before the night was out.

Meantime the Italian put his flag of truce into his pocket, and disappeared, at a leisurely pace, among the sand-hills.

'They make honourable war,' said Northmour. 'They are all gentlemen and soldiers. For the credit of the thing, I wish we could change sides – you and I, Frank, and you too, Missy, my darling – and leave that being on the bed to some one else. Tut! Don't look shocked! We are all going post to what they call eternity, and may as well be above-board while there's time. As far as I'm concerned, if I could first strangle Huddlestone and then get Clara in my arms, I could die with some pride and satisfaction. And as it is, by God, I'll have a kiss!'

Before I could do anything to interfere, he had rudely embraced and repeatedly kissed the resisting girl. Next moment I had pulled him away with fury, and flung him heavily against the wall. He laughed long and loud, and I feared his wits had given way under the strain; for even in the best of days he had been a sparing and a quiet laugher.

'Now, Frank,' said he, when his mirth was somewhat appeased, 'it's your turn. Here's my hand. Good-bye; farewell!' Then, seeing me stand rigid and indignant, and holding Clara to my side: 'Man!' he broke out, 'are you angry? Did you think we were going to die with all the airs and graces of society? I took a kiss; I'm glad I had it; and now you can take another if you like, and square accounts.'

I turned from him with a feeling of contempt which I did not seek to dissemble.

'As you please,' said he. 'You've been a prig in life; a prig you'll die.'

And with that he sat down in a chair, a rifle over his knee, and amused himself with snapping the lock; but I could see that his ebullition of light spirits (the only one I ever knew him to display) had already come to an end, and was succeeded by a sullen, scowling humour.

All this time our assailants might have been entering the house, and we been none the wiser; we had in truth almost forgotten the danger that so imminently overhung our days. But just then Mr Huddlestone uttered a cry, and leaped from the bed.

I asked him what was wrong.

'Fire!' he cried. 'They have set the house on fire!'

Northmour was on his feet in an instant, and he and I ran through the door of communication with the study. The room was illuminated by a red and angry light. Almost at the moment of our entrance a tower of flame arose in front of the window, and with a tingling report, a pane fell inwards on the carpet. They had set fire to the lean-to outhouse, where Northmour used to nurse his negatives.

'Hot work,' said Northmour. 'Let us try in your old room.'

We ran thither in a breath, threw up the casement, and looked forth. Along the whole back wall of the pavilion piles of fuel had been arranged and kindled; and it is probable they had been drenched with mineral oil, for in spite of the morning's rain they all burned bravely. The fire had taken a firm hold already on the outhouse, which blazed higher and higher every moment; the back door was in the centre of a red-hot bonfire; the eaves we could see, as we looked upward, were already smouldering, for the roof overhung, and was supported by considerable beams of wood. At the same time, hot, pungent, and choking volumes of smoke began to fill the house. There was not a human being to be seen to right or left.

'Ah, well!' said Northmour, 'here's the end, thank God.'

And we returned to *My Uncle's Room*. Mr Huddlestone was putting on his boots, still violently trembling, but with an air of determination such as I had not hitherto observed. Clara stood close by him, with her cloak in both hands ready to throw about her shoulders, and a strange look in her eyes, as if she were half hopeful, half doubtful of her father.

'Well, boys and girls,' said Northmour, 'how about a sally? The oven is heating; it is not good to stay here and be baked and, for my part, I want to come to my hands with them, and be done.'

'There is nothing else left,' I replied.

And both Clara and Mr Huddlestone, though with a very different intonation, added, 'Nothing.'

As we went downstairs the heat was excessive, and the roaring of the fire filled our ears; and we had scarce reached the passage before the stairs window fell in, a branch of flame shot brandishing through the aperture, and the interior of the pavilion became lit up with that dreadful and fluctuating glare. At the same moment we heard the fall of something heavy and inelastic in the upper storey. The whole pavilion, it was plain, had gone alight like a box of matches, and now not only flamed sky-high to land and sea, but threatened with every moment to crumble and fall in about our ears.

Northmour and I cocked our revolvers. Mr Huddlestone, who had already refused a firearm, put us behind him with a manner of command.

'Let Clara open the door,' said he. 'So if they fire a volley, she will be protected. And in the meantime stand behind me. I am the scapegoat; my sins have found me out.'

I heard him, as I stood breathless by his shoulder, with my pistol ready, pattering off prayers in a tremulous, rapid whisper; and I confess, horrid as the thought may seem, I despised him for thinking of supplications in a moment so critical and thrilling. In the meantime, Clara, who was dead white, but still possessed her faculties, had displaced the barricade from the front door. Another moment, and she had pulled it open. Firelight and moonlight illuminated the links with confused and changeful lustre, and far away against the sky we could see a long trail of glowing smoke.

Mr Huddlestone, filled for the moment with a strength greater than his own, struck Northmour and myself a back-hander in the chest; and while we were thus for the moment incapacitated from action, lifting his arms above his head like one about to dive, he ran straight forward out of the pavilion.

'Here am I!' he cried – 'Huddlestone! Kill me, and spare the others!'

His sudden appearance daunted, I suppose, our hidden enemies; for Northmour and I had time to recover, to seize Clara between us, one by each arm, and to rush forth to his assistance, ere anything further had taken place. But scarce had we passed the threshold when there came near a dozen reports and flashes from every direction among the hollows of the links. Mr Huddlestone staggered, uttered a weird and freezing cry, threw up his arms over his head, and fell backward on the turf.

'*Traditore! Traditore!*' cried the invisible avengers.

And just then a part of the roof of the pavilion fell in, so rapid was the progress of the fire. A loud, vague, and horrible noise accompanied the collapse, and a vast volume of flame went soaring up to heaven. It must have been visible at that moment from twenty miles out at sea, from the shore at Graden Wester, and far inland from the peak of Graystiel, the most eastern summit of the Caulder Hills. Bernard Huddlestone, although God knows what were his obsequies, had a fine pyre at the moment of his death.

9

Tells How Northmour Carried Out His Threat

I should have the greatest difficulty to tell you what followed next after this tragic circumstance. It is all to me, as I look back upon it, mixed, strenuous, and ineffectual, like the struggles of a sleeper in a nightmare. Clara, I remember, uttered a broken sigh and would have fallen forward to earth had not Northmour and I supported her insensible body. I do not think we were attacked; I do not remember even to have seen an assailant; and I believe we deserted Mr Huddlestone without a glance. I only remember running like a man in a panic, now carrying Clara altogether in my own arms, now sharing her weight with Northmour, now scuffling confusedly for the possession of that dear burden. Why we should have made for my camp in the Hemlock Den, or how we reached it, are points lost for ever to my recollection. The first moment at which I became definitely sure, Clara had been suffered to fall against the outside of my little tent, Northmour and I were tumbling together on the ground, and he, with contained ferocity, was striking for my head with the butt of his revolver. He had already twice wounded me on the scalp; and it is to the consequent loss of blood that I am tempted to attribute the sudden clearness of my mind.

I caught him by the wrist.

'Northmour,' I remember saying, 'you can kill me afterwards. Let us first attend to Clara.'

He was at that moment uppermost. Scarcely had the words passed my lips, when he had leaped to his feet and ran towards the tent; and the next moment he was straining Clara to his heart and covering her unconscious hands and face with his caresses.

'Shame!' I cried. 'Shame to you, Northmour!'

And, giddy though I still was, I struck him repeatedly upon the head and shoulders.

He relinquished his grasp, and faced me in the broken moonlight.

'I had you under, and I let you go,' said he; 'and now you strike me! Coward!'

'You are the coward,' I retorted. 'Did she wish your kisses while she was still sensible of what she wanted? Not she! And now she may be dying; and you waste this precious time, and abuse her helplessness. Stand aside, and let me help her.'

He confronted me for a moment, white and menacing; then suddenly he stepped aside.

'Help her then,' said he.

I threw myself on my knees beside her, and loosened, as well as I was able, her dress and corset; but while I was thus engaged, a grasp descended on my shoulder.

'Keep your hands off her,' said Northmour fiercely. 'Do you think I have no blood in my veins?'

'Northmour,' I cried, 'if you will neither help her yourself nor let me do so, do you know that I shall have to kill you?'

'That is better!' he cried. 'Let her die also, where's the harm? Step aside from that girl! and stand up to fight.'

'You will observe,' said I, half rising, 'that I have not kissed her yet.'

'I dare you to,' he cried.

I do not know what possessed me; it was one of the things I am most ashamed of in my life, though, as my wife used to say, I knew that my kisses would be always welcome were she dead or living; down I fell again upon my knees, parted the hair from her forehead, and, with the dearest respect, laid my lips for a moment on that cold brow. It was such a caress as a father might have given; it was such a one as was not unbecoming from a man soon to die to a woman already dead.

'And now,' said I, 'I am at your service, Mr Northmour.'

But I saw, to my surprise, that he had turned his back upon me. 'Do you hear?' I asked.

'Yes,' said he, 'I do. If you wish to fight, I am ready. If not, go on and save Clara. All is one to me.'

I did not wait to be twice bidden; but, stooping again

over Clara, continued my efforts to revive her. She still lay white and lifeless; I began to fear that her sweet spirit had indeed fled beyond recall, and horror and a sense of utter desolation seized upon my heart. I called her by name with the most endearing inflexions; I chafed and beat her hands; now I laid her head low, now supported it against my knee; but all seemed to be in vain, and the lids still lay heavy on her eyes.

'Northmour,' I said, 'there is my hat. For God's sake bring some water from the spring.'

Almost in a moment he was by my side with the water.

'I have brought it in my own,' he said. 'You do not grudge me the privilege?'

'Northmour,' I was beginning to say as I laved her head and breast; but he interrupted me savagely:

'Oh, you hush up!' he said. 'The best thing you can do is to say nothing.'

I had certainly no desire to talk, my mind being swallowed up in concern for my dear love and her condition; so I continued in silence to do my best towards her recovery, and, when the hat was empty, returned it to him, with one word – 'More.' He had, perhaps, gone several times upon this errand, when Clara re-opened her eyes.

'Now,' said he, 'since she is better, you can spare me, can you not? I wish you a good night, Mr Cassilis.'

And with that he was gone among the thicket. I made a fire, for I had now no fear of the Italians, who had even spared all the little possessions left in my encampment; and, broken as she was by the excitement and the hideous catastrophe of the evening, I managed in one way or another – by persuasion, encouragement, warmth, and such simple remedies as I could lay my hand on – to bring her back to some composure of mind and strength of body.

Day had already come, when a sharp 'Hist!' sounded from the thicket. I started from the ground but the voice of Northmour was heard adding, in the most tranquil tones: 'Come here, Cassilis, and alone; I want to show you something.'

I consulted Clara with my eyes, and, receiving her tacit permission, left her alone, and clambered out of the den. At some distance off I saw Northmour leaning against an elder; and, as soon as he perceived me, he began walking seaward. I had almost overtaken him as he reached the outskirts of the wood.

'Look,' said he, pausing.

A couple of steps more brought me out of the foliage. The light of the morning lay cold and clear over that well-known scene. The pavilion was but a blackened wreck; the roof had fallen in, one of the gables had fallen out; and, far and near, the face of the links was cicatrized with little patches of burnt furze. Thick smoke still went straight upwards in the windless air of the morning, and a great pile of ardent cinders filled the bare walls of the house, like coals in an open grate. Close by the islet a schooner yacht lay to, and a well-manned boat was pulling vigorously for the shore.

'The *Red Earl*!' I cried. 'The *Red Earl* twelve hours too late!'

'Feel in your pocket, Frank. Are you armed?' asked Northmour.

I obeyed him, and I think I must have become deadly pale. My revolver had been taken from me.

'You see I have you in my power,' he continued. 'I disarmed you last night while you were nursing Clara; but this morning – here – take your pistol. No thanks!' he cried, holding up his hand. 'I do not like them; that is the only way you can annoy me now.'

He began to walk forward across the links to meet the boat, and I followed a step or two behind. In front of the pavilion I paused to see where Mr Huddlestone had fallen; but there was no sign of him, nor so much as a trace of blood.

'Graden Floe,' said Northmour.

He continued to advance till we had come to the head of the beach.

'No farther, please,' said he. 'Would you like to take her to Graden House?'

'Thank you,' replied I; 'I shall try to get her to the minister's at Graden Wester.'

The prow of the boat here grated on the beach, and a sailor jumped ashore with a line in his hand.

'Wait a minute, lads!' cried Northmour; and then lower and to my private ear. 'You had better say nothing of all this to her,' he added.

'On the contrary,' I broke out, 'she shall know everything that I can tell.'

'You do not understand,' he returned, with an air of great dignity. 'It will be nothing to her; she expects it of me. Good-bye!' he added, with a nod.

I offered him my hand.

'Excuse me,' said he, 'it's small, I know; but I can't push things quite so far as that. I don't wish any sentimental business, to sit by your hearth a white-haired wanderer, and all that. Quite the contrary: I hope to God I shall never again clap eyes on either one of you.'

'Well, God bless you, Northmour!' I said heartily.

'Oh, yes,' he returned.

He walked down the beach; and the man who was ashore gave him an arm on board, and then shoved off and leaped into the bows himself. Northmour took the tiller; the boat rose to the waves, and the oars between the thole-pins sounded crisp and measured in the morning air.

They were not yet half-way to the *Red Earl*, and I was still watching their progress, when the sun rose out of the sea.

One more word and my story is done. Years after, Northmour was killed fighting under the colours of Garibaldi for the liberation of the Tyrol.

MARTIN AMIS · *God's Dice*
HANS CHRISTIAN ANDERSEN · *The Emperor's New Clothes*
MARCUS AURELIUS · *Meditations*
JAMES BALDWIN · *Sonny's Blues*
AMBROSE BIERCE · *An Occurrence at Owl Creek Bridge*
DIRK BOGARDE · *From Le Pigeonnier*
WILLIAM BOYD · *Killing Lizards*
POPPY Z. BRITE · *His Mouth will Taste of Wormwood*
ITALO CALVINO · *Ten Italian Folktales*
ALBERT CAMUS · *Summer*
TRUMAN CAPOTE · *First and Last*
RAYMOND CHANDLER · *Goldfish*
ANTON CHEKHOV · *The Black Monk*
ROALD DAHL · *Lamb to the Slaughter*
ELIZABETH DAVID · *I'll be with You in the Squeezing of a Lemon*
N. J. DAWOOD (TRANS.) · *The Seven Voyages of Sindbad the Sailor*
ISAK DINESEN · *The Dreaming Child*
SIR ARTHUR CONAN DOYLE · *The Man with the Twisted Lip*
DICK FRANCIS · *Racing Classics*
SIGMUND FREUD · *Five Lectures on Psycho-Analysis*
KAHLIL GIBRAN · *Prophet, Madman, Wanderer*
STEPHEN JAY GOULD · *Adam's Navel*
ALASDAIR GRAY · *Five Letters from an Eastern Empire*
GRAHAM GREENE · *Under the Garden*
JAMES HERRIOT · *Seven Yorkshire Tales*
PATRICIA HIGHSMITH · *Little Tales of Misogyny*
M. R. JAMES AND R. L. STEVENSON · *The Haunted Dolls' House*
RUDYARD KIPLING · *Baa Baa, Black Sheep*
PENELOPE LIVELY · *A Long Night at Abu Simbel*
KATHERINE MANSFIELD · *The Escape*